'Our passion
was so great.
Will the Old
Man understand
and help us
once again?'

SHEN FU

Born 1763, Jiangsu province, China

Selection taken from *Six Records of a Floating Life*,
written in 1809 and discovered in the 1870s.

SHEN FU IN PENGUIN CLASSICS
Six Records of a Floating Life

SHEN FU

The Old Man of the Moon

Translated by
Leonard Pratt and Chiang Su-hui

PENGUIN BOOKS

PENGUIN CLASSICS

Published by the Penguin Group
Penguin Books Ltd, 80 Strand, London WC2R ORL, England
Penguin Group (USA) Inc., 375 Hudson Street, New York, New York 10014, USA
Penguin Group (Canada), 90 Eglinton Avenue East, Suite 700, Toronto, Ontario,
Canada M4P 2Y3 (a division of Pearson Penguin Canada Inc.)
Penguin Ireland, 25 St Stephen's Green, Dublin 2, Ireland
(a division of Penguin Books Ltd)
Penguin Group (Australia), 707 Collins Street, Melbourne, Victoria 3008, Australia
(a division of Pearson Australia Group Pty Ltd)
Penguin Books India Pvt Ltd, 11 Community Centre, Panchsheel Park,
New Delhi – 110 017, India
Penguin Group (NZ), 67 Apollo Drive, Rosedale, Auckland 0632, New Zealand
(a division of Pearson New Zealand Ltd)
Penguin Books (South Africa) (Pty) Ltd, Block D, Rosebank Office Park,
181 Jan Smuts Avenue, Parktown North, Gauteng 2193, South Africa

Penguin Books Ltd, Registered Offices: 80 Strand, London WC2R ORL, England

www.penguin.com

This selection published in Penguin Classics 2015
001

Translation copyright © Leonard Pratt, 1983

The moral right of the translator has been asserted

Set in 9.5/13 pt Baskerville 10 Pro
Typeset by Jouve (UK), Milton Keynes
Printed in Great Britain by Clays Ltd, St Ives plc

A CIP catalogue record for this book is available from the British Library

ISBN: 978–0–141–39780–1

www.greenpenguin.co.uk

MIX
Paper from
responsible sources
FSC
www.fsc.org FSC™ C018179

Penguin Books is committed to a sustainable
future for our business, our readers and our planet.
This book is made from Forest Stewardship
Council™ certified paper.

I was born in the winter of the 27th year of the reign of the Emperor Chien Lung, on the second and twentieth day of the eleventh month. Heaven blessed me, and life then could not have been more full. It was a time of great peace and plenty, and my family was an official one that lived next to the Pavilion of the Waves in Soochow. As the poet Su Tung-po wrote, 'All things are like spring dreams, passing with no trace.' If I did not make a record of that time, I should be ungrateful for the blessings of heaven.

The very first of the three hundred chapters of the *Book of Odes* concerns husbands and wives, so I too will write of other matters in their turn. Unfortunately I never completed my studies, so my writing is not very skilful. But here my purpose is merely to record true feelings and actual events. Criticism of my writing will be like the shining of a bright light into a dirty mirror.

When I was young I was engaged to Chin Sha-yu, but she died when she was eight years old. Eventually I married Chen Yün, the daughter of my uncle, Mr Chen Hsin-yü. Her literary name was Shu-chen.

Even while small, she was very clever. While she was learning to talk she was taught the poem *The Mandolin Song* and could repeat it almost immediately.

Yün's father died when she was four years old, leaving her mother, whose family name was Chin, and her younger brother, Ko-chang. At first they had virtually nothing, but as Yün grew older she became very adept at needlework, and the labour of her ten fingers came to provide for all three of them. Thanks to her work, they were always able to afford to pay the tuition for her brother's teachers.

One day Yün found a copy of *The Mandolin Song* in her brother's book-box and, remembering her lessons as a child, was able to pick out the characters one by one. That is how she began learning to read. In her spare moments she gradually learned how to write poetry, one line of which was, 'We grow thin in the shadows of autumn, but chrysanthemums grow fat with the dew.'

When I was thirteen, my mother took me along on a visit to her relatives. That was the first time I met my cousin Yün, and we two children got on well together. I had a chance to see her poems that day, and though I sighed at her brilliance I privately feared she was too sensitive to be completely happy in life. Still, I could not forget her, and I remember saying to my mother, 'If you are going to choose a wife for me, I will marry no other than Yün.'

Mother also loved her gentleness, so she was quick to

arrange our engagement, sealing the match by giving Yün a gold ring from her own finger. This was in the 39th year of the reign of the Emperor Chien Lung, on the 16th day of the seventh month.

That winter mother took me to their home once again, for the marriage of Yün's cousin. Yün and I were born in the same year, but because she was ten months older than I, I had always called her 'elder sister', while she called me 'younger brother'. We continued to call one another by these names even after we were engaged.

At her cousin's wedding the room was full of beautifully dressed people. Yün alone wore a plain dress; only her shoes were new. I noticed they were skilfully embroidered, and when she told me she had done them herself I began to appreciate that her cleverness lay not only in her writing.

Yün had delicate shoulders and a stately neck, and her figure was slim. Her brows arched over beautiful, lively eyes. Her only blemish was two slightly protruding front teeth, the sign of a lack of good fortune. But her manner was altogether charming, and she captivated all who saw her.

I asked to see more of her poems that day, and found some had only one line, others three or four, and most were unfinished. I asked her why.

'I have done them without a teacher,' she replied, laughing. 'I hope you, my best friend, can be my teacher now and help me finish them.' Then as a joke I wrote on her book, 'The Embroidered Bag of Beautiful Verses'. I did not then realize that the origin of her early death already lay in that book.

That night after the wedding I escorted my relatives out of the city, and it was midnight by the time I returned. I was terribly hungry and asked for something to eat. A servant brought me some dried plums, but they were too sweet for me. So Yün secretly took me to her room, where she had hidden some warm rice porridge and some small dishes of food. I delightedly picked up my chopsticks, but suddenly heard Yün's cousin Yu-heng call, 'Yün, come quickly!'

Yün hurriedly shut the door and called back, 'I'm very tired. I was just going to sleep.' But Yu-heng pushed open the door and came in anyway.

He saw me just about to begin eating the rice porridge, and chuckled, looking out of the corner of his eye at Yün. 'When I asked you for some rice porridge just now, you said there wasn't any more! But I see you were just hiding it in here and saving it for your "husband"!'

Yün was terribly embarrassed, and ran out. The whole household broke into laughter. I was also embarrassed and angry, roused my servant, and left early.

Every time I returned after that, Yün would hide. I knew she was afraid that everyone would laugh at her.

On the night of the 22nd day of the first month in the 44th year of the reign of the Emperor Chien Lung I saw by the light of our wedding candles that Yün's figure was as slim as before. When her veil was lifted we smiled at each other. After we had shared the ceremonial cup of wine and sat down together for the wedding banquet, I secretly took her small hand under the table. It was warm and it was soft, and my heart beat uncontrollably.

I asked her to begin eating, but it turned out to be a day on which she did not eat meat, a Buddhist practice which she had followed for several years. I thought to myself that she had begun this practice at the very time I had begun to break out with acne, and I asked her, 'Since my skin is now clear and healthy, couldn't you give up this custom?' Her eyes smiled amusement, and her head nodded agreement.

That same night of the 22nd there was a wedding-eve party for my elder sister. She was to be married on the 24th, but the 23rd was a day of national mourning on which all entertaining was forbidden and the holding of the wedding-eve party would have been impossible. Yün attended the dinner, but I spent the time in our bedroom drinking with my sister's maid of honour. We played a drinking game which I lost frequently, and I wound up getting very drunk and falling asleep. By the time I woke up the next morning, Yün was already putting on her make-up.

During the day a constant stream of relatives and friends came to congratulate Yün and me on our marriage. In the evening there were some musical performances in honour of the wedding, after the lamps had been lit.

At midnight I escorted my sister to her new husband's home, and it was almost three in the morning when I returned. The candles had burned low and the house was silent. I stole quietly into our room to find my wife's servant dozing beside the bed and Yün herself with her make-up off but not yet asleep. A candle burned brightly beside her; she was bent intently over a book, but I could not tell what it was that she was reading with such concentration. I went up to her, rubbed her shoulder, and said, 'You've been so busy these past few days, why are you reading so late?'

Yün turned and stood up. 'I was just thinking of going to sleep, but I opened the bookcase and found this book, *The Romance of the Western Chamber*. Once I had started reading it, I forgot how tired I was. I had often heard it spoken of, but this was the first time I had had a chance to read it. The author really is as talented as people say, but I do think his tale is too explicitly told.'

I laughed and said, 'Only a talented writer could be so explicit.'

Yün's servant then urged us to go to sleep, but we told her she should go to sleep first, and to shut the door to our room. We sat up making jokes, like two close friends meeting after a long separation. I playfully felt her breast and found her heart was beating as fast as mine. I pulled her to me and whispered in her ear, 'Why is your heart beating so fast?' She answered with a bewitching smile that made me feel a love so endless it shook my soul. I held her close as I parted the curtains and led her into bed. We never noticed what time the sun rose in the morning.

As a new bride, Yün was very quiet. She never got angry, and when anyone spoke to her she always replied with a smile. She was respectful to her elders and amiable to everyone else. Everything she did was orderly, and was done properly. Each morning when she saw the first rays of the sun touch the top of the window, she would dress quickly and hurry out of bed, as if someone were calling her. I once laughed at her about it; 'This is not like that time with the rice porridge! Why are you still afraid of someone laughing at you?'

'True,' she answered, 'my hiding the rice porridge for you that time has become a joke. But I'm not worried about people laughing at me now. I am afraid your parents will think I'm lazy.'

While I would have liked it if she could have slept more, I had to agree that she was right. So every morning I got up early with her, and from that time on we were inseparable, like a man and his shadow. Words could not describe our love.

We were so happy that our first month together passed in the twinkling of an eye. At that time my father, the Honourable Chia-fu, was working as a private secretary in the prefectural government office at Kuichi. He sent for me, having enrolled me as a student of Mr Chao Sheng-chai at Wulin. Mr Chao taught me patiently and well; the fact that I can write at all today is due to his efforts.

I had, however, originally planned to continue my studies with my father after my marriage, so I was disappointed when I received his letter. I feared Yün would weep when she heard of it, but she showed no emotion, encouraged me to go, and helped me pack my bag. The night before I left she was slightly subdued, but that was all. When it was time for me to go, though, she whispered to me, 'There will be no one there to look after you. Please take good care of yourself.'

My boat cast off just as the peach and the plum flowers were in magnificent bloom. I felt like a bird that had lost its flock. My world was shaken. After I arrived at the offices where my father worked, he immediately began preparations to go east across the river.

Our separation of three months seemed as if it were ten years long. Yün wrote to me frequently, but her letters asked about me twice as often as they told me anything about herself. Most of what she wrote was merely to encourage me in my studies, and the rest was just polite chatter. I really was a little angry with her. Every time the wind would rustle the bamboo trees in the yard, or the moon would shine through the leaves of the banana tree outside my window, I would look out and miss her so terribly that dreams of her took possession of my soul.

My teacher understood how I felt, and wrote to tell my

father about it. He then assigned me ten compositions and sent me home for a while to write them. I felt like a prisoner who has been pardoned.

Once I was on the boat each quarter of an hour seemed to pass as slowly as a year. After I got home and paid my respects to my mother, I went into our room and Yün rose to greet me. She held my hands without saying a word. Our souls became smoke and mist. I thought I heard something, but it was as if my body had ceased to exist.

It was then the sixth month, and steamy hot in our room. Fortunately we lived just west of the Pavilion of the Waves' Lotus Lovers' Hall, where it was cooler. By a bridge and overlooking a stream there was a small hall called My Desire, because, as desired, one could 'wash my hat strings in it when it is clean, and wash my feet in it when it is dirty'. Almost under the eaves of the hall there was an old tree that cast a shadow across the windows so deep that it turned one's face green. Strollers were always walking along the opposite bank of the stream. This was where my father, the Honourable Chia-fu, used to entertain guests privately, and I obtained my mother's permission to take Yün there to escape the summer's heat. Because it was so hot, Yün had given up her embroidery. She spent all day with me as I studied, and we talked of ancient times, analysed the moon, and discussed the flowers. Yün could not take much drink, and would accept at the most three cups of wine when I forced her to. I taught her a literary game, in which the

9

loser has to drink a cup. We were certain two people had never been happier than we were.

One day Yün asked me, 'Of all the ancient literary masters, who do you think is the best?'

'*The Annals of the Warring States* and *Chuang Tsu* are known for their liveliness,' I replied. 'Kuang Heng and Liu Hsiang are known for their elegance. Shih Chien and Pan Ku are known for their breadth. Change Li is known for his extensive knowledge, and Liu Chou for his vigorous style. Lu Ling is known for his originality, and Su Hsün and his two sons for their essays. There are also the policy debates of Chia and Tung, the poetic styles of Yü and Hsü, and the Imperial memorials of Lu Chih. I could never give a complete list of all the talented writers there have been. Besides, which one you like depends upon which one you feel in sympathy with.'

'It takes great knowledge and a heroic spirit to appreciate ancient literature,' said Yün. 'I fear a woman's learning is not enough to master it. The only way we have of understanding it is through poetry, and I understand but a bit of that.'

'During the Tang Dynasty all candidates had to pass an examination in poetry before they could become officials,' I remarked. 'Clearly the best were Li Pai and Tu Fu. Which of them do you like best?'

Yün said her opinion was that 'Tu Fu's poetry is very pure and carefully tempered, while Li Pai's is ethereal and open. Personally, I would rather have Li Pai's liveliness than Tu Fu's strictness.'

'But Tu Fu was the more successful, and most scholars prefer him. Why do you alone like Li Pai?'

'Tu Fu is alone,' Yün replied, 'in the detail of his verse and the vividness of his expression. But Li Pai's poetry flows like a flower tossed into a stream. It's enchanting. I would not say Li Pai is a better poet than Tu Fu, but only that he appeals to me more.'

I smiled and said, 'I never thought you were such an admirer of Li Pai's.'

Yün smiled back. 'Apart from him, there is only my first teacher, Mr Pai Lo-tien. I have always had a feeling in my heart for him that has never changed.'

'Why do you say that?' I asked.

'Didn't he write *The Mandolin Song?*'

I laughed. 'Isn't that strange! You are an admirer of Li Pai's, and Pai Lo-tien was your first tutor. And as it happens, the literary name of your husband is San-pai. What is this affinity you have for the character *pai?*'

Yün laughed and said, 'Since I do have an affinity for the character *pai*, I'm afraid that in the future my writing will be full of *pai* characters.' (Our Kiangsu accent pronounces the character *pieh* as *pai*.) We both shook with laughter.

'Since you know poetry,' I said, 'you must know the good and bad points of the form called *fu*.'

'I know it's descended from the ancient Chu Tzu

poetry,' Yün replied, 'but I have only studied it a little and it's hard to understand. Of the *fu* poets of the Han and Chin Dynasties, who had the best meter and the most refined language, I think Hsiang-ju was the best.'

I jokingly said, 'So perhaps Wen-chün did not fall in love with Hsiang-ju because of the way he played the lute after all, but because of his poetry?' The conversation ended with us both laughing loudly.

I am by nature candid and unconstrained, but Yün was scrupulous and meticulously polite. When I would occasionally put a cape over her shoulders or help her adjust her sleeves, she would invariably say, 'I beg your pardon.' If I gave her a handkerchief or a fan, she would always stand to take it. At first I did not like her acting like this, and once I said to her, 'Do you think that by being so polite you can make me do as you like? For it is said that "Deceit hides behind too much courtesy".'

Yün blushed. 'Why should respect and good manners be called deceit?'

'True respect comes from the heart, not from empty words,' I said.

'There is no one closer to us than our parents,' Yün said, arguing with me now. 'But how could we merely respect them in our hearts while being rude in our treatment of them?'

'But I was only joking,' I protested.

'Most arguments people have begin with a joke,' Yün

said. 'Don't ever argue with me for the fun of it again – it makes me so angry I could die!'

I pulled her close to me, patted her back, and comforted her. Her anger passed and she began to smile. From then on, the polite phrases 'How dare I?' and 'I beg your pardon' became mere expressions to us. We lived together with the greatest mutual respect for three and twenty years, and as the years passed we grew ever closer.

Whenever we would meet one another in a darkened room or a narrow hallway of the house, we would hold hands and ask, 'Where are you going?' We felt furtive, as if we were afraid others would see us. In fact, at first we even avoided being seen walking or sitting together, though after a while we thought nothing of it. If Yün were sitting and talking with someone and saw me come in, she would stand up and move over to me and I would sit down beside her. Neither of us thought about this and it seemed quite natural; and though at first we felt embarrassed about it, we gradually grew accustomed to doing it. The strangest thing to me then was how old couples seemed to treat one another like enemies. I did not understand why. Yet people said, 'Otherwise, how could they grow old together?' Could this be true? I wondered.

On the evening of the 7th day of the seventh month that year, Yün lit candles and set out fruit on the altar by the Pavilion of My Desire, and we worshipped Tien Sun together. I had had two matching seals engraved with the inscription, 'May we remain husband and wife in all our lives to come'; on mine the characters were raised and on hers they were incised. We used them to sign the letters we wrote one another. That night the moonlight was very lovely, and as it was reflected in the stream it turned the ripples of the water as white as silk. We sat together near the water wearing light robes and fanned ourselves gently as we looked up at the clouds flying across the sky and changing into ten thousand shapes.

Yün said, 'The world is so vast, but still everyone looks up at the same moon. I wonder if there is another couple in the world as much in love as we are.'

'Naturally there are people everywhere who like to enjoy the night air and gaze at the moon,' I said, 'and there are more than a few women who enjoy discussing the sunset. But when a man and wife look at it together, I don't think it is the sunset they will wind up talking about.' The candles soon burned out, and the moon set. We took the fruit inside and went to bed.

The 15th day of the seventh month, when the moon is full, is the day called the Ghost Festival. Yün had prepared some small dishes, and we had planned to invite the moon to drink with us. But when night came, clouds suddenly darkened the sky.

Yün grew melancholy and said, 'If I am to grow old together with you, the moon must come out.'

I also felt depressed. On the opposite bank I could see will-o'-the-wisps winking on and off like ten thousand fireflies, as their light threaded through the high grass and willow trees that grew on the small island in the stream. To get ourselves into a better mood Yün and I began composing a poem out loud, with me offering the first couplet, her the second, and so on. After the first two couplets we gradually became less and less restrained and more and more excited, until we were saying anything that came into our heads. Yün was soon laughing so hard that she cried, and had to lean up against me, unable to speak a word. The heavy scent of jasmine in her hair assailed my nostrils, so to stop her laughing I patted her on the back and changed the subject, saying, 'I thought women of ancient times put jasmine flowers in their hair because they resembled pearls. I never realized that the jasmine is so attractive when mixed with the scent of women's make-up, much more attractive than the lime.'

Yün stopped laughing. 'Lime is the gentleman of perfumes,' she said, 'and you notice its scent unconsciously. But the jasmine is a commoner that has to rely on a woman's make-up for its effect. It's suggestive, like a wicked smile.'

'So why are you avoiding the gentleman and taking up with the commoner?'

'I'm only making fun of gentlemen who love commoners,' she replied.

Just as we were speaking, the water clock showed midnight. The wind gradually began to sweep the clouds away, and the full moon finally came out. We were delighted, and drank some wine leaning against the windowsill. But before we had finished three cups we heard a loud noise from under the bridge, as if someone had fallen into the water. We leaned out of the window and looked around carefully. The surface of the stream was as bright as a mirror, but we saw not a thing. We only heard the sound of a duck running quickly along the river bank. I knew that the ghosts of people who had drowned often appeared by the river near the Pavilion of the Waves, but I was worried that Yün would be afraid and so I did not dare tell her.

'Yi!' she said, none the less frightened for my silence. 'Where did that sound come from?'

We could not keep ourselves from trembling. I closed the window and we took the wine into the bedroom. The flame in the lamp was as small as a bean, and the curtains around the bed cast shadows that writhed like snakes. We were still frightened. I turned up the lamp and we got into bed, but Yün was already suffering hot and cold attacks from the shock. I caught the same fever, and we were ill for twenty days. It is true what people say, that happiness carried to an extreme turns into sadness. The events of that day were another omen that we were not to grow old together.

By the time of the Mid-Autumn Festival I had just started to feel better, though I was still a little weak. Yün had by this time been my wife for half a year without once going next door to the Pavilion of the Waves, so one evening I sent an old servant there to tell the gate-keeper not to let in any other visitors. Just as night was falling, Yün, my little sister, and I walked there. Two servants helped me along and another led the way. We crossed the stone bridge, went in at the gate, and took a small winding path along the eastern side of the gardens. There were rocks piled up into small artificial mountains, and trees with luxuriant light green leaves. The pavilion itself stood on top of a small hill. Steps led up to the summit, from where you could see all around for several miles. The smoke of cooking fires rose up from every direction into the brilliant twilight. On the opposite bank was a place called Chinshan Woods, where high officials would hold formal banquets; at that time the Chengyi Academy had not yet been established there. We had taken along a blanket which we spread out in the middle of the pavilion, and we all sat around in a circle on it, while the gate-keeper made tea and brought it up to us. A full moon soon rose above the trees, and we gradually felt a breeze beginning to tug at our sleeves. The moon shone on the stream below, and quickly drove away our cares.

'This is such fun!' said Yün. 'Wouldn't it be wonderful if we had a small skiff to row around in the stream down there?'

The time had come to light the lanterns, so, still thinking of the shock we had received on the night of the Ghost Festival, we left the pavilion and went home, holding

17

hands all the way. It is a Soochow custom that on the night of the Mid-Autumn Festival women, regardless of whether they come from a well-off family or not, all come out in groups to stroll. This is called the 'moonlight walk'. But although the Pavilion of the Waves was elegant and peaceful, no one had come there that night.

My father, the Honourable Chia-fu, liked to adopt sons, so I had twenty-six brothers with surnames different from mine. My mother too had adopted nine daughters; Miss Wang, the second of them, and Miss Yü, the sixth, got on best with Yün. Miss Wang was a simple girl who enjoyed drinking, while Miss Yü was open and loved to talk. Every time they got together they would exile me so that the three of them could sleep in the same bed. This was Miss Yü's idea.

'After you are married,' I once joked with her, 'I will invite your husband over and make him stay at least ten days.'

'I'll come along too,' she replied, 'and sleep with your wife. Won't that be fun?' Yün and Miss Wang said nothing, but only smiled.

At the time of my younger brother Chi-tang's marriage, we moved to Granary Lane, near the Drinking Horses Bridge. Although the new house was big, it was not as elegant as the one near the Pavilion of the Waves. For my mother's birthday that year we had an opera troupe come to perform, and Yün at first thought it was quite wonderful. My father had never been superstitious, however, so

he had no compunctions about asking for the performance of *The Sad Parting*. The actors were excellent and,
watching it, we were very moved.

But while the performance was still going on, I saw
Yün suddenly get up from behind the screen where the
women were seated and go to our room. After a long
while she had still not returned, so I went in to look for
her, Miss Yü and Miss Wang following me. We found Yün
sitting alone beside the dressing table with her head in
her hands.

'Are you unhappy about something?' I asked her.

'Seeing an opera is supposed to be entertaining,' Yün
said. 'But today's is heartbreaking.'

Both Miss Yü and Miss Wang were laughing at her, but
I told them they had to understand what a very emotional
person she was. Still, Miss Yü asked her, 'Are you going
to sit here by yourself all day?'

'When there's something I like, I'll go back and watch
it,' Yün replied. Miss Wang went out as soon as she'd
heard this, and asked my mother to tell them to perform
things like *Tse Liang* and *Hou So*. After some urging Yün
came out to watch, and soon began to cheer up.

My father's cousin, the Honourable Su-tsun, died
young leaving no descendants, so my father named me
to inherit from him. His grave was on ancestral ground
at Hsikuatang on the Mountain of Prosperity and Lon-
gevity, and every spring I had to take Yün there to sweep
the grave and perform the rites. Second sister Wang had

heard of a beautiful place on the mountain called the Ko
Garden, and so she once asked to go along with us.

That day Yün saw some stones on the mountainside
that were streaked with beautiful colours. 'If we put some
in a bowl to make a little mountain,' she said, 'they would
look even better than white stones from Hsüanchou.'

I told Yün I feared it would be hard to find enough
stones to do that, but Miss Wang volunteered to collect
them. She immediately went to the grave-keeper and borrowed a hempen bag, and then began collecting the
stones, walking along as slowly and as deliberately as a
crane. She would pick up each one, and if I said 'good'
she would keep it; if I said 'no', she would throw it away.

Before long she was perspiring heavily and, dragging
her bag, she came back to us and said, 'I don't have the
strength to pick up any more.'

'I've heard that if you want to collect fruit in the mountains,' said Yün as she selected the stones she wanted,
'you have to get a monkey to do it for you. Now I know
that that's true!'

Miss Wang rubbed her hands together furiously, as if
she were going to tickle Yün in revenge for her joke. I
stood between them to stop her, and scolded Yün. 'Miss
Wang has been working while you've been relaxing, and
still you talk like that. No wonder she's angry.'

On the way back we strolled through the Ko Garden,
where the fresh, light green leaves and the delicate red
flowers seemed to be competing over which was the most

beautiful. Miss Wang always had been a foolish girl, and as soon as she saw the flowers she thought she had to pick some. Yün scolded her. 'You have no vase to put them in, and you're not going to put them in your hair either. Why are you picking so many?'

'They feel no pain,' Miss Wang said, 'so what's the harm?'

I laughed and told her, 'You are going to marry a pock-marked, hairy fellow. That will be the flowers' revenge.'

Miss Wang looked at me angrily, threw the flowers on the ground, and kicked them into a pond with her tiny foot. 'How can you make fun of me like this?' she said. But Yün joked with her, and her anger passed.

When we were first married Yün was very quiet, and enjoyed listening to me discuss things. But I drew her out, as a man will use a blade of grass to encourage a cricket to chirp, and she gradually became able to express herself, as the following conversation proves.

Every day Yün would mix her rice with tea. She liked to eat a spicy, salty kind of beancurd that Soochow people call 'stinking beancurd'. She also liked pickled cucumber. These last two were things I had hated all my life, so one day I said to her, 'Dogs have no stomach, and eat dung because they do not realize how bad it smells. A beetle rolls in its dung so it can become a cicada, because it wants to fly as high as it can. Which are you, a dog or a beetle?'

'That kind of beancurd is cheap,' Yün said, 'and it tastes good with either rice porridge or plain rice. I've eaten it since I was a child. As I am now living in your home I'm like the beetle that has become a cicada, and the reason I still like to eat the beancurd is that I have not forgotten my former life. As for pickled cucumber, the first time I had it was here in your home.'

'In other words, my house is a doghouse?' I said, continuing to joke with her.

Yün was embarrassed and quickly explained. 'There is dung in every house. The only question is whether one eats it. I don't like garlic, but I still eat it because you like it. I would never ask you to eat stinking beancurd; but as for pickled cucumber, if you would only hold your nose and eat some you would realize how good it is. It's like the old stories about the girl named Wu-yen, who was ugly but virtuous.'

'Now are you trying to get me to behave like a dog?'

'I've been acting like a dog for a long time,' Yün said. 'Why don't you try it?' Upon which she picked up a piece of pickled cucumber with her chopsticks and forced it into my mouth. I held my nose and chewed, and it did seem quite good. I took my hand away and continued chewing, and to my surprise found it did have rather a special taste. From then on, I too began to enjoy eating it.

Yün also ate salted beancurd by pouring sesame seed oil and a little sugar over it, and that was wonderful. She would sometimes eat the beancurd by mixing it with a paste of pickled cucumber; this she called 'double-delicious sauce', and it was very good.

One day I said to her, 'At first I did not like any of these things, but now I have come to like all of them very much. I cannot understand why.'

'If you like something,' said Yün, 'you don't care if it's ugly.'

My younger brother Chi-tang's wife is the granddaughter of Wang Hsü-chou. As the time for their marriage approached, she discovered she did not have enough pearl flowers. Yün took out her own pearls that she had been given when we were married, and gave them to my mother for her to give to my brother's fiancée. The servants thought it was a pity that she should give up her own jewellery.

'Women are entirely *yin* in nature,' Yün told them, 'and pearls are the essence of *yin*. If you wear them in your hair, they completely overcome the spirit of *yang*. So why should I value them?'

On the other hand, she prized shabby old books and tattered paintings. She would take the partial remnants of old books, separate them all into sections by topic, and then have them rebound. These she called her 'Fragments of Literature'. When she found some calligraphy or a painting that had been ruined, she felt she had to search for a piece of old paper on which to remount it. If there were portions missing, she would ask me to restore them. These she named the 'Collection of Discarded Delights'.

23

Yün would work on these projects the whole day without becoming tired, whenever she could take time off from her sewing and cooking. If, in an old trunk or a shabby book, she came across a piece of paper with something on it, she acted as if she had found something very special. Every time our neighbour, old lady Fung, got hold of some scraps of old books, she would sell them to Yün.

Yün's habits and tastes were the same as mine. She understood what my eyes said, and the language of my brows. She did everything according to my expression, and everything she did was as I wished it.

Once I said to her, 'It's a pity that you are a woman and have to remain hidden away at home. If only you could become a man we could visit famous mountains and search out magnificent ruins. We could travel the whole world together. Wouldn't that be wonderful?'

'What is so difficult about that?' Yün replied. 'After my hair begins to turn white, although we could not go so far as to visit the Five Sacred Mountains, we could still visit places nearer by. We could probably go together to Hufu and Lingyen, and south to the West Lake and north to Ping Mountain.'

'By the time your hair begins to turn white, I'm afraid you will find it hard to walk,' I told her.

'Then if we can't do it in this life, I hope we will do it in the next.'

'In our next life I hope you will be born a man,' I said. 'I will be a woman, and we can be together again.'

'That would be lovely,' said Yün, 'especially if we could still remember this life.'

I laughed. 'We still haven't finished talking about that business with the rice porridge when we were young. If in the next life we can still remember this one, we will have so much to talk about on our wedding night that we will never get to sleep!'

'People say that marriages are arranged by the "Old Man of the Moon",' said Yün. 'He has already pulled us together in this life, and in the next we will have to depend on him too. Why don't we have a picture of him painted so we can worship him?'

At that time the famous portraitist Chi Liu-ti, whose literary name was Chun, was living in Tiaohsi, and we asked him to paint the picture for us. He portrayed the old man carrying his red silk cord in one hand, while with the other he grasped his walking stick with the *Book of Marriages* tied to the top of it. Though his hair was white, his face was that of a child, and he was striding through mist and fog. This was the best painting that Mr Chi ever did. My friend Shih Cho-tang wrote a complimentary inscription at the top of the painting, and I hung it in our room. On the 1st and the 15th days of each month, Yün and I would light incense and worship in front of it. Later, because of the many things that happened to our family, the painting was somehow lost and I have no idea in whose home it hangs now. 'Our next life is not known, while this life closes.' Our passion was so great. Will the Old Man understand and help us once again?

After we moved to Granary Lane, I called our upstairs bedroom the Pavilion of My Guest's Fragrance, after Yün's name and the idea that husbands and wives should treat each other like guests. The new house had only a small garden and high walls, and there was nothing much that we liked about it. At the back there was a row of small rooms off the library, but when their windows were open there was nothing to see but the overgrown Lu Family Garden, which was a desolate sight. It was from this time that Yün began to miss the scenery of the Pavilion of the Waves.

There was then an old woman who lived east of the Chinmu Bridge and north of Keng Lane. Her cottage was surrounded by a vegetable garden, and had a rattan gate. Outside the gate there was a pond about one *mou* in size that reflected the interwoven images of the flowers and the shadows of the trees. The place was the site of the ruins of the palace that Chang Shih-cheng had built at the end of the Yüan Dynasty. Immediately to the west of her house there was a pile of broken bricks as big as a small hill, and if you climbed to the top you could see for a long way, a large area with few people and great wild beauty. The old woman once spoke of the place to Yün, who wanted very much to go and see it. 'Since we left the Pavilion of the Waves,' she told me, 'I dream about it night and day. As we cannot go back there, the only thing

I can think of now is trying to find a substitute for it. What about this old woman's house?'

'In the worst heat of the early autumn,' I said, 'I think every morning of having a cool place to pass the long days. If you're interested, I'll have a look first and see whether the house is habitable. If it is, we could take our bedding and stay there for a month. What would you think of that?'

'I'm afraid your parents will disapprove,' Yün said.

I told her I would ask their permission myself, and the next day I went to look over the house. It had only two rooms, one in front and one at the back, each divided by a partition. The windows were paper and the bed of bamboo, and the place had altogether a subtle charm about it. When the old woman heard what we wanted, she was very happy to rent the bedroom to us. I pasted white paper up on the walls, and soon it looked like a different place entirely. I then respectfully informed my mother, and took Yün to live there.

Our only neighbours were an old couple who raised vegetables for a living. Learning we had come to escape the summer's heat, they came to call on us, bringing gifts of fish from the pond and vegetables from the garden. I tried to pay for them, but they would not take anything, so Yün made them some shoes, which we finally prevailed on them to accept.

It was then the beginning of the seventh month, with dark shadows among the green trees. There was a breeze across the water, and the songs of cicadas were every-where. The old couple also made us a fishing pole, and I took Yün fishing in the deep shadows of the willow trees.

When the sun was going down, we would climb to the top of the small hill and admire the twilight. We used to make up impromptu poems there, one line of which was, 'Beast-like clouds eat the setting sun, the bow-like moon shoots falling stars.' After a while, when the moonlight fell directly into the pond and the sound of insects came from all around, we would move the bed out beside the fence. The old woman would come to tell us when the wine was warm and the food was hot. We would drink in the moonlight until we were a little tipsy, and then eat. After having a wash, we would fan ourselves with banana leaves, and sit or lie down and listen to our old neigh-bours telling stories of sin and retribution. At three strokes of the night watch we would go in to sleep feeling cool and refreshed. It was almost like not living in the city at all.

We had asked the old couple to buy chrysanthemums and plant them all the way around the fence, and when the flowers bloomed in the ninth month I decided to stay there with Yün for ten more days. About then my mother came to visit us, and seemed quite happy with what she saw. We ate crabs beside the flowers, and thoroughly enjoyed the day.

'One day we should build a cottage here and buy ten

mou of land to make a garden around it,' said Yün happily. 'We could have servants plant melons and vegetables that would be enough to live on. What with your painting and my embroidery, it would give us enough to have a little to drink while we wrote poetry. We could live quite happily wearing cotton clothes and eating nothing but vegetables and rice. We would never have to leave here.' I deeply wished we could do so. The cottage is still there, but now I have lost my most intimate friend. It is enough to make one sigh deeply.

About half a *li* from my house, on Vinegar Warehouse Lane, was the Tungting Temple, which we usually called the Narcissus Temple. Inside there were winding covered paths and a small park with pavilions. Every year on the god's birthday the members of each family association would gather in their corner of the temple, hang up a special glass lantern, and erect a throne below it. Beside the throne they would set out vases filled with flowers, in a competition to see whose decorations were most beautiful. During the day operas were performed, and at night candles of different lengths were set out among the vases and the flowers. This was called the 'lighting of the flowers'. The colours of the flowers, the shadows of the lamps, and the fragrant smoke floating up from the incense urns, made it all seem like a night banquet at the palace of the Dragon King himself. The heads of the family associations would play the flute and sing, or brew fine tea and chat with one another. Townspeople gathered like ants to watch this spectacle, and a fence had to be put up under the eaves of the temple to keep them out.

One year some friends of mine invited me to go and help to arrange their flowers, so I had a chance to see the festival myself. I went home and told Yün how beautiful it was.

'What a shame that I cannot go just because I am not a man,' said Yün.

'If you wore one of my hats and some of my clothes, you could look like a man.'

Yün thereupon braided her hair into a plait and made up her eyebrows. She put on my hat, and though her hair showed a little around her ears it was easy to conceal. When she put on my robe we found it was an inch and a half too long, but she took it up around the waist and put on a riding jacket over it.

'What about my feet?' Yün asked.

'In the street they sell "butterfly shoes",' I said, 'in all sizes. They're easy to buy, and afterwards you can wear them around the house. Wouldn't they do?'

Yün was delighted, and when she had put on my clothes after dinner she practised for a long time, putting her hands into her sleeves and taking large steps like a man.

But suddenly she changed her mind. 'I am not going! It would be awful if someone found out. If your parents knew, they would never allow us to go.'

I still encouraged her to go, however. 'Everyone at the temple knows me. Even if they find out, they will only take it as a joke. Mother is at ninth sister's house, so if we come and go secretly no one will ever know.'

Yün looked at herself in the mirror and laughed endlessly. I pulled her along, and we left quietly. We walked all around inside the temple, with no one realizing she was a woman. If someone asked who she was, I would tell them she was my cousin. They would only fold their hands and bow to her.

At the last place we came to, young women and girls were sitting behind the throne that had been erected there. They were the family of a Mr Yang, one of the organizers of the festival. Without thinking, Yün walked over and began to chat with them as a woman quite naturally might, and as she bent over to do so she inadvertently laid her hand on the shoulder of one of the young ladies.

One of the maids angrily jumped up and shouted, 'What kind of a rogue are you, to behave like that!' I went over to try to explain, but Yün, seeing how embarrassing the situation could become, quickly took off her hat and kicked up her foot, saying, 'See, I am a woman too!'

At first they all stared at Yün in surprise, but then their anger turned to laughter. We stayed to have some tea and refreshments with them, and then called sedan chairs and went home.

* * *

In the seventh month of the Chiayen year of the reign of the Emperor Chien Lung I returned from Yüehtung with my friend Hsü Hsiu-feng, who was my cousin's husband. He brought a new concubine back with him, raving about her beauty to everyone, and one day he invited Yün to go and see her. Afterwards Yün said to Hsiu-feng, 'She certainly is beautiful, but she is not the least bit charming.'

'If your husband were to take a concubine,' Hsiu-feng asked, 'would she have to be charming as well as beautiful?'

'Naturally,' said Yün.

From then on, Yün was obsessed with the idea of finding me a concubine, even though we had nowhere near enough money for such an ambition.

There was a courtesan from Chekiang named Wen Leng-hsiang then living in Soochow. She was something of a poet, and had written four stanzas on the theme of willow catkins that had taken the city by storm, many talented writers composing couplets in response to her originals. My friend from Wuchiang, Chang Hsien-han, had long admired Leng-hsiang, and asked us to help him write some verses to accompany hers. Yün thought little of her and so declined, but I longed to write, and thus composed some verses to her rhyme. One couplet that Yün liked very much was, 'They arouse my springtime wistfulness, and ensnare her wandering fancy.'

A year later, on the 5th day of the eighth month, mother was planning to take Yün on a visit to Tiger Hill, when my friend Hsien-han suddenly arrived at our house. 'I am going to Tiger Hill too,' he said, 'and today I came especially to invite you to go with me and admire some flowers along the way.'

I then asked mother to go on ahead, and said I would meet her at Pantang near Tiger Hill. Hsien-han took me to Leng-hsiang's home, where I discovered that she was already middle-aged.

However, she had a daughter named Han-yüan, who, though not yet fully mature, was as beautiful as a piece of jade. Her eyes were as lovely as the surface of an autumn pond, and while they entertained us it became obvious that her literary knowledge was extensive. She had a younger sister named Wen-yüan who was still quite small.

At first I had no wild ideas and wanted only to have a cup of wine and chat with them. I well knew that a poor scholar like myself could not afford this sort of thing, and once inside I began to feel quite nervous. While I did not show my unease in my conversation, I did quietly say to Hsien-han 'I'm only a poor fellow. How can you invite these girls to entertain me?'

Hsien-han laughed. 'It's not that way at all. A friend of mine had invited me to come and be entertained by Han-yüan today, but then he was called away by an important visitor. He asked me to be the host and invite someone else. Don't worry about it.'

At that, I began to relax. Later, when our boat reached Pantang, I told Han-yüan to go aboard my mother's boat and pay her respects. That was when Yün met Han-yüan and, as happy as old friends at a reunion, they soon set off hand in hand to climb the hill in search of all the scenic spots it offered. Yün especially liked the height and vista of Thousand Clouds, and they sat there enjoying the view for some time. When we returned to Yehfangpin, we moored the boats side by side and drank long and happily.

As the boats were being unmoored, Yün asked me if Han-yüan could return aboard hers, while I went back with Hsien-han. To this, I agreed. When we returned to the Tuting Bridge we went back aboard our own boats and took leave of one another. By the time we arrived home it was already the third night watch.

'Today I have met someone who is both beautiful and charming,' said Yün. 'I have just invited Han-yüan to come and see me tomorrow, so I can try to arrange things for you.'

'But we're not a rich family,' I said, worried. 'We cannot afford to keep someone like that. How could people as poor as ourselves dare think of such a thing? And we are so happily married, why should we look for someone else?'

'But I love her too,' Yün said, laughing. 'You just let me take care of everything.'

The next day at noon, Han-yüan actually came. Yün entertained her warmly, and during the meal we played a game – the winner would read a poem, while the loser had to drink a cup of wine. By the end of the meal still not a word had been said about our obtaining Han-yüan.

As soon as she left, Yün said to me, 'I have just made a secret agreement with her. She will come here on the 18th, and we will pledge ourselves as sisters. You will have to prepare animals for the sacrifice.'

Then, laughing and pointing to the jade bracelet on her arm, she said, 'If you see this bracelet on Han-yüan's arm then, it will mean she has agreed to our proposal. I have just told her my idea, but I am still not very sure what she thinks about it all.'

I only listened to what she said, making no reply.

It rained very hard on the 18th, but Han-yüan came all the same. She and Yün went into another room and were alone there for some time. They were holding hands when they emerged, and Han-yüan looked at me shyly. She was wearing the jade bracelet!

We had intended, after the incense was burned and they had become sisters, that we should carry on drinking. As it turned out, however, Han-yüan had promised to go on a trip to Stone Lake, so she left as soon as the ceremony was over.

'She has agreed,' Yün told me happily. 'Now, how will you reward your go-between?' I asked her the details of the arrangement.

'Just now I spoke to her privately because I was afraid she might have another attachment. When she said she did not, I asked her, "Do you know why we have invited you here today, little sister?"

' "The respect of an honourable lady like yourself makes

35

me feel like a small weed leaning up against a great tree,"
she replied, "but my mother has high hopes for me, and
I'm afraid I cannot agree without consulting her. I do
hope, though, that you and I can think of a way to work
things out."

'When I took off the bracelet and put it on her arm I
said to her, "The jade of this bracelet is hard and repre-
sents the constancy of our pledge; and like our pledge,
the circle of the bracelet has no end. Wear it as the first
token of our understanding." To which she replied, "The
power to unite us rests entirely with you." So it seems as
if we have already won over Han-yüan. The difficult part
will be convincing her mother, but I will think of a plan
for that.'

I laughed, and asked her, 'Are you trying to imitate
Li-weng's *Pitying the Fragrant Companion*?'

'Yes,' she replied.

From that time on there was not a day that Yün did not
talk about Han-yüan. But later Han-yüan was taken off
by a powerful man, and all the plans came to nothing. In
fact, it was because of this that Yün died.

* * *

Yün had had the blood sickness ever since her younger
brother Ko-chang had run away from home and her
mother had missed him so much that she died of grief.
Yün was so distraught she had fallen ill herself. From the
time she met Han-yüan, she passed no blood for over a

year, and I was delighted that Yün had found such a good
cure in her friend, when Han-yüan was snatched away by
an influential man who paid a thousand golds for her and
also promised to take care of her mother. 'The beauty
belongs to Sha-shih-li!' I had learned of all this but had
not dared to say anything to Yün, so she did not find out
about it until one day when she went to see Han-yüan.
She returned weeping, and said, 'I had not thought Han's
feelings could be so shallow!'

'Your own feelings are too deep,' I said. 'How can that
sort of person be said to have feelings? Someone who is
used to beautiful clothes and delicate foods could never
grow accustomed to thorn hairpins and plain cloth
dresses. It's better that we should be unsuccessful now
than to have her regret things later.'

I comforted her repeatedly, but having been so
wounded Yün still suffered great discharges of blood. She
was bedridden and did not respond to any treatment. She
suffered relapses, and became so thin you could see her
bones. After a few years the money we owed increased
daily, and so did the gossip about us. And because she
had pledged sisterhood with a sing-song girl, my parents'
scorn for Yün deepened daily. I became the mediator
between my parents and my wife. It was no way to live!

Yün had given birth to a girl named Ching-chün, who
by then was fourteen years old. She could read and write
well and was also very capable, so fortunately we could
rely on her help in pawning hairpins and clothes. Our

37

son was named Feng-sen; at this time he was twelve years old and was studying reading with a teacher. I was then without employment for several years, so I had opened up a shop in our home, selling books and paintings. But I did not make enough in three days to pay the expenses of one. I was weary and beset by hardships, and we often had no money. In the deepest winter I had no furs, but there was nothing to do but to be strong and bear the cold. Ching-chün, too, shivered in an unlined dress, though she bravely denied being cold. On account of this, Yün swore she would never spend the money to see a doctor or buy medicine.

Once during a period when Yün was able to get out of bed, it happened that my friend Chou Chun-hsi had just returned from Prince Fu's secretariat and wanted to hire someone to embroider the Heart Sutra for him. Yün thought that by embroidering a sutra she might bring us some luck to ease our difficulties, as well as getting a good price for her work, so despite her illness she agreed to do it. As it turned out Chun-hsi was only on a quick visit and could not wait long, needing the job completed in ten days. Yün was still weak, and the sudden work made her waist hurt and gave her dizzy spells. Who would have thought her fate was so bad that even the Buddha would not show her mercy! After she had embroidered the sutra, her illness worsened. First she would call for water, then she would want soup. The family began to grow weary of her.

There was a Westerner who had rented the house to the left of my painting shop. He made his living by lending out money at interest, and I had come to know him when he asked me to do paintings for him. A friend of mine had once borrowed fifty golds from him, asking me to be the guarantor. I would have been embarrassed to refuse and so agreed to it, but then he ended up by running off with the loan. The Westerner had only me to ask for repayment, and often came to demand his money. At first I gave him paintings in lieu of payment, but gradually I came to have nothing left to give him. At the end of the year while my father was at home, he came again to demand repayment, and made a commotion at the gate.

When my father heard the noise he called for me and scolded me angrily, saying, 'We are a house of robes and caps. How could we owe money to someone like this!'

Just as I was about to explain, a messenger arrived. He had been sent by a woman who had been a sworn sister of Yün's as a child, who had married a man named Hua from Hsishan, and who had heard of her illness and wanted to inquire after her.

My father, however, mistakenly thought he was a messenger from Han-yüan and so became even angrier, saying, 'Your wife does not behave as a woman should, swearing sisterhood with a sing-song girl. Nor do you think to learn from your elders, running around with riff-raff. I cannot bear to send you to the execution ground, but I will give you only three days. Make plans to leave home, and make them quickly. If you take longer, you will lose your head for your disobedience!'

When Yün heard this she wept, and said, 'It is all my fault that father is so angry. Yet if I committed suicide and you left home, you could not bear it; and if I stayed here while you left, you could not stand it. Go secretly and tell the messenger from the Huas to come here. I will force myself to get out of bed and talk to him.'

I told Ching-chün to help her out of the bedroom, and fetched the messenger from the Huas. 'Did your mistress send you here specially,' Yün asked, 'or did you come because you just happened to be passing this way?'

The messenger replied, 'My mistress had heard of madam's illness some time ago, and originally wanted to come personally to visit you. But because she had never entered your gate before, she did not dare to come herself. As I was leaving she told me to say that if madam does not mind a plain and rustic life, she could come and build up her strength in the countryside, according to the pledge they made to one another under the lamplight when they were young.' This last referred to a pledge Yün and she had made once when they were embroidering together, to help one another if they were ever ill.

So Yün told him to go home quickly and ask his mistress to send a boat for us secretly two days later.

After he left, Yün said to me, 'Sister Hua is closer to me than my own flesh and blood. If you don't mind moving to her home, we can go there together. I'm afraid we won't be able to take the children with us, though, and we certainly cannot leave them here to trouble our parents. We will have to make arrangements for them in the next two days.'

At that time my cousin Wang Chin-chen had a son named Yün-shih and wanted to have Ching-chün for his daughter-in-law. 'I hear young Wang is timid and without much ability,' said Yün, 'and that while he will be able to keep up what the Wangs own, they do not own much to keep up. On the other hand, they are a respectable family and have only the one son. I think we should allow the marriage.'

I met with Chin-chen and said, 'My father and you have the friendship of Weiyang. If you want Ching-chün for your daughter-in-law I do not think he will refuse you. But she must be brought up a little longer before she is ready for marriage, and in the circumstances we will not be able to do that. After my wife and I have gone to Hsishan, how would you feel about going to my parents and asking for her first to be your child daughter-in-law?' He happily agreed to my suggestion.

I also made arrangements for our son Feng-sen, asking my friend Hsia Yi-shan to introduce him to someone from whom he could learn the business of trading. This was no sooner done than the Huas' boat arrived. It was then the 25th day of the twelfth month of 1800.

Yün said to me, 'Since we are leaving alone, I am afraid that not only will the neighbours laugh at us, but also

41

that the Westerner will not let us go as we still cannot repay his loan. We must go quietly tomorrow morning at the fifth night watch.'

'But you are ill,' I protested. 'Can you stand the morning cold?'

'Life and death are governed by fate,' Yün replied. 'Do not worry about me.'

I secretly informed my father of what we were going to do, and he agreed to it. That night I first carried a little baggage down to the boat on a shoulder pole, and then told Feng-sen to go to sleep. Ching-chün was crying at her mother's side.

These were Yün's parting instructions to our daughter: 'Your mother has had a bitter fate and emotions that run too deep; therefore we have had these many problems. Fortunately your father has been kind to me, and there is nothing to worry about in our leaving. In two or three years we will be able to arrange for us all to be reunited. Go to your new home, behave as a proper woman in everything you do, and do not be like your mother. Your father-in-law and mother-in-law will be happy to have you, and will surely treat you well. You can take with you all the cases, boxes, and anything else we have left behind. Your little brother is still young, so we have not told him what we are doing. When we are about to leave, we will tell him that I am going to see a doctor and will be back in a few days; after we have left, explain everything to him, and let grandfather take care of him.'

At our side was the old woman who had once rented us her house so that we could escape the summer's heat. She wanted to go with us to the countryside, and since she could not she stood beside us wiping away her tears. Just before the striking of the fifth night watch we all ate some warm rice porridge.

Yün laughed bravely. 'Once it was rice porridge that brought us together,' she said, 'and now it is rice porridge that sends us away. If someone wrote a play about it, he could call it *The Romance of the Rice Porridge*.'

Feng-sen heard her talking and woke up, saying sleepily, 'What are you doing, mother?'

'I am going out to see a doctor,' Yün replied.

'Why so early?'

'Because it is far away. You and elder sister should stay home and be good. Do not make grandmother angry. I am going with your father and will be back in a few days.'

As the cock crowed three times, Yün, with tears in her eyes and her arm around the old woman, was just opening the back door to go out when Feng-sen cried loudly, 'Yi! My mother is not coming back!'

Ching-chün feared he would awaken others, so she quickly covered his mouth with her hand and comforted him. By this time Yün and I felt as if we were being torn apart, but there was nothing more we could say. We could only tell him not to cry.

After Ching-chün shut the door, Yün was able to walk only about a dozen steps from our lane before she was

43

too tired to go any farther. We continued with me carrying Yün on my back and the old woman holding up the lantern. We had nearly reached the boat when we were almost arrested by a night patrolman, but fortunately the servant woman told him that Yün was her daughter who was ill and that I was her son-in-law. When the boatmen (who all worked for the Hua family) heard us talking, they came to meet us and helped us down to the boat. After we cast off Yün finally burst out crying, and wept bitterly. After this separation, mother and son never saw each other again.

Hua was named Ta-cheng, and he lived facing the mountains at Tungkaoshan in Wuhsi. He farmed the land himself, and was very simple and sincere. His wife – Yün's sworn sister – was from the Hsia family. It was early in the afternoon of that day before we arrived at their house. Madam Hua had been waiting for us by the gate, and when we arrived she led her two small daughters to the boat to greet us. Everyone was very happy to see us. Yün was helped ashore and we were treated very hospitably. After a while the neighbours' wives burst into the room along with their children, and stood around Yün looking her over. Some asked her questions, some offered her condolences, while others whispered to one another, all filling the house with the sound of their chatter.

Yün told Madam Hua, 'Today I feel just like the fisherman who wandered into Peach Blossom Spring!'

'Please don't laugh at our country folk,' replied

Mrs Hua. 'That which they seldom see they consider most wonderful.'

Thus we settled down to pass the New Year. Only two score days after we arrived, by the Festival of the First Moon, Yün was starting to be able to get up and around. That night as we watched the dragon lanterns on the threshing floor, her spirits began to revive. I then began to feel at peace myself, and decided to talk our situation over with her. 'We have no future living here,' I said, 'but we are too short of money to go anywhere else. What do you think we should do?'

'I have been thinking about this too,' said Yün. 'Your elder sister's husband Fan Hui-lai is now chief accountant at the Chingchiang Salt Office. Ten years ago when he wanted to borrow ten golds from you we did not have the money and I pawned my hairpins to get it. Do you remember?'

'I had forgotten!'

'I hear Chingchiang is not far away. Why don't you go and see if he can help us?'

I did as she suggested. At the time it was very warm, and I felt the heat even dressed only in a woollen gown and a worsted short jacket. This was the 16th day of the first month of 1801. That night I spent at an inn at Hsishan, where I rented bedding.

The next morning I took a boat for Chiangyin, but the winds were against us and there was a continuous drizzle. By the time we reached the river mouth at Chiangyin the spring cold was cutting me to the bone. I bought some wine to ward off the cold, but that exhausted my purse. All night I tried to decide whether I should sell my undergarments to get money for the ferry.

By the 19th the north wind was stronger and the snow was deeper everywhere. I could not hold back bitter tears. Alone, I worked out lodging and ferry expenses, and did not dare to buy any more to drink. I was trembling in soul and body when an old man suddenly entered the inn, wearing straw sandals and a felt hat and carrying a yellow bag on his back. He looked at me as if he knew me.

'Aren't you Tsao from Taichou?' I asked.

'I am,' he replied, 'and if it were not for you I would be lying dead in a ditch by now! My little girl is well, and she often sings your praises. What a surprise to meet you today! What are you hanging about here for?'

Now when I was working in the government offices at Taichou there was this same Tsao, a poor man with a beautiful daughter who had already been betrothed. But then a man of some influence had loaned him money in a plan to obtain his daughter, and it had all led to legal proceedings. I had helped protect them and send his daughter back to her betrothed. In his gratitude, Tsao had volunteered as a servant at the *yamen* and kowtowed to me, and so I had come to know him. I told him how I had been going to see my brother-in-law and had run into the snowstorm.

'I am heading that way myself,' Tsao said. 'If the

weather clears tomorrow I will take you there.' Then he took out money to buy wine, and was most courteous to me.

On the 20th, as soon as the monastery's morning bells began to ring, I heard the ferryman's shouts by the river mouth. I got up in a hurry and called to Tsao to come along. 'Don't be in such a rush,' he said. 'We should eat our fill before boarding the boat.'

Then he paid for my room and my meals, and took me off to buy something for breakfast. I had been delayed for days, and was anxious to get across on the ferry, so I did not feel like eating, but I forced down two sesame cakes. As we boarded the boat, the river wind cut through our garments like an arrow, and soon I was trembling in all four limbs.

'I hear a Chiangyin man has hung himself in Chingchiang,' said Tsao, 'and that his wife has chartered this boat to go there. We have to wait for her before we can cross.' I had to wait until noon before we cast off, still hungry and fighting the cold. By the time we reached Chingchiang the smoke from evening cooking fires was rising on all sides.

'There are two *yamen* at Chingchiang,' said Tsao. 'Is the man you are visiting at the one inside the wall or the one outside the wall?'

Staggering along behind him, I confessed I did not know. 'Then we might just as well stop here for the night,' Tsao said, 'and go to look for him tomorrow.'

My shoes and stockings were filthy with mud and wet through, so at the inn that night I asked to dry them by the fire. I gulped down a meal and fell into an exhausted sleep, however, so that by the time I awoke the next day my stockings were half burned.

That morning Tsao once again paid for my room and board. We arrived at the *yamen* inside the wall to find that Hui-lai had not yet got up, but on hearing that I had arrived he threw on some clothes and came out. Seeing the state I was in, he was very upset; 'What calamity has brought you here?' he asked.

'Just a moment,' I said. 'First, have you got two golds you can loan me to repay the man who brought me here?'

Hui-lai gave me two barbarian cakes and I offered them to Tsao. He was determined to refuse them, but finally accepted one and left. I then told Hui-lai everything that had happened, and why I had come.

'You and I are relatives by marriage,' he said, 'and even if there were no old debt I should do everything I could for you. But unfortunately our sea-going salt boats have just been taken by pirates. We are now trying to straighten out the accounts, and I have no means of finding the money. The best I could do would be to give you twenty coins of barbarian silver to repay the debt. Would that be all right?'

I had not had any extravagant hopes to begin with, so I accepted. I stayed on two more days, but when the sky cleared and the weather turned warmer I made plans to go back, returning to the Huas on the 25th.

Yün asked whether I had run into the snow, and I told her about my ordeal. 'When it snowed I thought you had already reached Chingchiang,' she said sadly, 'but you were still held up at the river mouth. You were lucky to run into old Tsao. It's true that heaven watches over the good.'

Several days later we received a letter from Ching-chün telling us that Yi-shan had already found Feng-sen a job in a shop. Chin-chen had asked permission of my father and on the 24th day of the first month had taken Ching-chün to his home. Our children's affairs seemed well in order, but we were still sad at being parted from them.

By the beginning of the second month the sun was warmer and the wind less strong, and with the money I had got at Chingchiang I made some simple preparations to visit my old friend Hu Ken-tang at the Hanchiang Salt Bureau. There was a tax office there, where I succeeded in obtaining a position as secretary, after which body and soul were a little more settled.

In the eighth month of the next year, 1802, I received a letter from Yün saying, 'My illness is now completely cured. I don't think it is a good idea for me to live and board indefinitely at a home where I have neither relatives nor friends. I would like to join you at Hanchiang, and see the glory of Ping Mountain.'

After receiving this letter I rented a house of two spans facing the river outside the Hsienchun Gate at

Hanchiang, and went myself to the Huas to fetch Yün. Madam Hua presented us with a child servant called Ah Shuang, to help with housework and meals, and we agreed that one day we should all be neighbours. By this time it was already the tenth month, and bitterly cold on Ping Mountain, so Yün and I decided not to go there until spring.

With Yün recovered we were happy again, and full of hope that we could reunite our family. But before the month was out the tax bureau suddenly cut its staff by fifteen persons, and as I was only the friend of a friend, I was dismissed. At first Yün still managed to come up with a hundred plans for us, putting on a brave front to comfort me. Never did she in the least find fault, though by the second month of spring, 1803, she began to suffer great discharges of blood once again. I wanted to return to Chingchiang and beg my brother-in-law for more help, but, as Yün put it, 'It's better to ask for help from a friend than from a relative.'

'That's true,' I replied, 'but all our friends are now out of work as well. While they may be concerned about us, they could not help us if they wanted to.'

'Then fortunately the weather at least has turned warm,' said Yün, 'so you won't have to worry about the road being blocked by snow. Please go quickly, come back as soon as you can, and don't worry about my being ill. If anything were to happen to you, my sins would be even heavier.'

Our income was irregular, but so that Yün would not worry I pretended to her that I was hiring a mule. In fact I walked, with some cakes in my bag and eating as I went. I headed south-east for about eighty or ninety *li*, twice taking a ferry across a forked river, and finally coming to a district where I could see no villages in any direction. I walked on until it grew late, but still saw only endless stretches of yellow sand and bright, twinkling stars. Finally I came to an earth god shrine, about five feet tall and surrounded by a low wall. A pair of cypress trees was planted beside it.

I kowtowed to the god and said a prayer. 'My name is Shen and I am from Soochow. I am going to visit relatives, but have lost my way. Let me borrow your temple for a night's rest. Blessed spirit, protect me.'

I then moved aside the small stone incense pot and squeezed myself into the shrine. It was big enough for only half my body, so I turned my wind cap around to cover my face and lay half inside the shrine with my knees sticking out. I shut my eyes and listened quietly, but the only sound was the whistling of the wind. With my feet tired and my spirits weak, I collapsed into sleep.

When I awoke it was already light in the east, and suddenly I heard the sound of walking and talking outside the wall. I rushed out to see who it was, and it turned out to be some local people passing by on their way to market. I asked the way to Chingchiang, and one of them told me, 'Go south ten *li* and you will come to the county seat at Taihsing City. Go straight through the town and then head east for another ten *li*, when you will come to an earthen mound. Pass eight of these mounds and you will come to Chingchiang. All these places are along the main road.'

I went back inside the shrine to return the incense pot to its original position, then kowtowed my thanks to the god and left. After passing through Taihsing I was able to take a wheelbarrow, and arrived at Chingchiang about four o'clock in the afternoon. I sent my calling card in to my brother-in-law's office, but only after a long while did the gate-keeper come out and tell me, 'His Honour Mr Fan has gone to Changchou on business.'

From the way he spoke, this sounded like an excuse. 'When will he be back?' I asked.

'I don't know.'

'Then I will wait for him,' I said, 'even if I have to wait a year.'

The gate-keeper saw that I meant what I said, and quietly asked me, 'Is His Honour Mr Fan's mother-in-law really your mother?'

'If she were not, I would not be waiting for Mr Fan to come back!'

'Then you just wait for him,' the gate-keeper said. After three days I was told Hui-lai had returned, and was given twenty-five golds. I hired a mule and hurried home.

I returned to find Yün moaning and weeping, looking as if something awful had happened. As soon as she saw me she burst out, 'Did you know that yesterday noon Ah Shuang stole all our things and ran away? I have asked people to search everywhere, but they still have not found him. Losing our things is a small matter, but what of our relationship with our friends? As we were leaving, his mother told me over and over again to take good care of him. I'm terribly worried he's running back home and will have to cross the Great River. And what will we do if his parents have hidden him to blackmail us? How can I face my sworn sister again?'

'Please calm down,' I said. 'You've been worrying about it too much. You can only blackmail someone who has money; with you and me, it's all our four shoulders can do to support our two mouths. Besides, in the half year the boy has been with us, we have given him clothing and shared our food with him. Our neighbours all know we have never once beaten him or scolded him. What's really happened is that the wretched child has ignored his conscience and taken advantage of our problems to run away with our belongings. Your sworn sister at the Huas' gave us a thief. How can you say you cannot face her? It is she who should not be able to face you. What we should do now is report this case to the magistrate, so as to avoid any questions being raised about it in the future.'

After Yün heard me speak, her mind seemed somewhat eased, but from then on she began frequently to talk in her sleep, calling out, 'Ah Shuang has run away!' or 'How could Han-yüan turn her back on me?' Her illness worsened daily.

Finally I was about to call a doctor to treat her, but she stopped me. 'My illness began because of my terribly deep grief over my brother's running away and my mother's death,' said Yün. 'It continued because of my affections, and now it has returned because of my indignation. I have always worried too much about things, and while I have tried my best to be a good daughter-in-law, I have failed.

'These are the reasons why I have come down with dizziness and palpitations of the heart. The disease has already entered my vitals, and there is nothing a doctor can do about it. Please do not spend money on something that cannot help.

'I have been happy as your wife these twenty-three years. You have loved me and sympathized with me in everything, and never rejected me despite my faults. Having had for my husband an intimate friend like you, I have no regrets over this life. I have had warm cotton clothes, enough to eat, and a pleasant home. I have strolled among streams and rocks, at places like the Pavilion of the Waves and the Villa of Serenity. In the midst of life, I have been just like an Immortal. But a true Immortal must go through many incarnations before reaching enlightenment. Who could dare hope to become an Immortal in only one lifetime? In our eagerness for immortality, we have only incurred the wrath of the Creator, and brought on our troubles with our passion. Because you have loved me too much, I have had a short life!'

Later she sobbed and spoke again. 'Even someone who lives a hundred years must still die one day. I am only sorry at having to leave you so suddenly and for so long, halfway through our journey. I will not be able to serve you for all your life, or to see Feng-sen's wedding with my own eyes.' When she finished, she wept great tears.

I forced myself to be strong and comforted her saying, 'You have been ill for eight years, and it has seemed critical many times. Why do you suddenly say such heartbreaking things now?'

'I have been dreaming every night that my parents have sent a boat to fetch me,' said Yün. 'When I shut my eyes it feels as if I'm floating, as if I were walking in the mist. Is my spirit leaving me, while only my body remains?'

'That is only because you are upset,' I said. 'If you will relax, drink some medicine, and take care of yourself, you will get better.'

Yün only sobbed again and said, 'If I thought I had the slightest thread of life left in me I would never dare alarm you by talking to you like this. But the road to the next world is near, and if I do not speak to you now there will never be a day when I can.

'It is all because of me that you have lost the affection of your parents and drifted apart from them. Do not worry, for after I die you will be able to regain their hearts. Your parents' springs and autumns are many, and when I die you should return to them quickly. If you cannot take my bones home, it does not matter if you leave my coffin here for a while until you can come for it. I also want you to find someone who is attractive and capable, to serve our parents and bring up my children. If you will do this for me, I can die in peace.'

When she had said this a great sad moan forced itself from her, as if she was in an agony of heartbreak.

'If you part from me half way I would never want to take another wife,' I said. 'You know the saying, "One who has seen the ocean cannot desire a stream, and compared with Wu Mountain there are no clouds anywhere."'

Yün then took my hand and it seemed there was something else she wanted to say, but she could only brokenly repeat the two words 'next life'. Suddenly she fell silent and began to pant, her eyes staring into the distance. I called her name a thousand times, but she could not speak. Two streams of agonized tears flowed from her eyes in torrents, until finally her panting grew shallow and her tears dried up. Her spirit vanished in the mist and she began her long journey. This was on the 30th day of the third month in the 7th year of the reign of the Emperor Chia Ching. When it happened there was a solitary lamp burning in the room. I looked up but saw nothing, there was nothing for my two hands to hold, and my heart felt as if it would shatter. How can there be anything greater than my everlasting grief?

My friend Hu Ken-tang loaned me ten golds, and by

selling every single thing remaining in the house I put together enough money to give my beloved a proper burial.

Alas! Yün came to this world a woman, but she had the feelings and abilities of a man. After she entered the gate of my home in marriage, I had to rush about daily to earn our clothing and food, there was never enough, but she never once complained. When I was living at home, all we had for entertainment was talk about literature. What a pity that she should have died in poverty and after long illness. And whose fault was it that she did? It was my fault, what else can I say? I would advise all the husbands and wives in the world not to hate one another, certainly, but also not to love too deeply. As it is said, 'An affectionate couple cannot grow old together.' My example should serve as a warning to others.